THE CYMAGE

ANDLIOS ORIGINS

DAVE WALSH

This is a work of fiction. Names, characters, places and incidents are either the product of the author's imagination or are used fictitiously, and any resemblance to any persons, living or dead, business establishments, events or locales is entirely coincidental.

THE CYMAGE

Edited by: Amanda West.

First ebook edition: June, 2019.

Printed in the United States of America

First Edition: June, 2019

Find out more about the author and his upcoming books at https://www. dvewlsh.com or @dvewlsh.

THE CYMAGE

DAVE WALSH

dvewlsh.com

ONE

THE PEDDLER AND THE JARL

The rain cascaded down in sheets, drops beating against the thin tin roof that sat over Am'ranth's head while he lugged another box from his workshop to his transport. This shipment was going directly to Jarl Quorthon himself, which was a great honor for a simple monk like Am'ranth. The rest of his brothers looked down upon his incessant tinkering, considering that the life of a Helgean was one of simplicity. The complications and technological advances of modern society were not a part of the Helgean lifestyle, but for Am'ranth it was difficult to quell that curiosity.

There were others like him scattered throughout the city of Cydonia on the planet Andlios, but most didn't have the knack for it quite like Am'ranth did. To the regulars of Cydonia they knew him as the "Peddler" for the stall he would set up in the market square every fortnight to sell his latest inventions. His inventions were trinkets, nothing groundbreaking or serious, and created out of pure wonder and curiosity, never for profit or from delusions of grandeur.

Somehow, though, he had caught the eye of Jarl Quorthon

on his last visit to Cydonia. Am'ranth was manning his makeshift booth made of an old table from the monastery with some rough spun cloth tossed over it, like he always was, a smile etched onto his sun-battered face. His stall stood ragged in the middle of the town square, the sand whipping through the streets where it weathered everything and everyone that stood in its path. Quorthon and his guard detail parted the crowd of the down-trodden and pious when they walked through the square, their opulence a contrast to the throngs of commoners. Quorthon and Am'ranth were different in just about every way: Am'ranth was short, with a light brown complexion, clean shaven, and short-cropped hair in the approved style for a Helgean monk, while Quorthon was tall and burly with flowing blonde locks and a beard to match. A thick pelt adorned Quorthon's shoulders, accenting the blend of traditional and modern Krigan style, while Am'ranth was in his robe and sandals.

"My good man." Quorthon stood towering over his booth, flanked by guards carrying blasters with large axes strapped to their backs. "What is it you sell?"

"Greetings, my lord," Am'ranth said, startled at the mere fact that the Jarl of Krigar was speaking with him. He stood an imposing, larger-than-life figure without a care in the world. "I'm but a mere Helgean monk and these are just some trinkets I've made."

"I see." The Jarl reached down and picked up a mechanical hábrók, inspecting the regal hawk before turning back to Am'ranth. "What exactly does this do?"

"You have an expert eye, my lord," Am'ranth said. "Simply press the button on the underside there and see for yourself."

"My lord." One of his guards stepped forward, only for

Quorthon to thrust his hand out at the man's chest, stopping him in his tracks.

"It's but a bird, Asger. I'm sure this fine man here has nothing sinister up his sleeve."

"Oh no, never, my lord." Am'ranth turned flush.

"So let us see here." He held the bird in his large right hand, inspecting the underside and pressing the button. "Oh, that is strange. I can feel it tugging at me a bit."

"Simply let go of it, my lord."

"By the Gods," he said after he released it from his grasp and it hovered in front of him. The wings were flapping as it hovered in place; it greatly amused the Jarl. "Will you look at that? How did you do this?"

"That isn't all, my lord." The anxiety melted away, giving in to his pride and curiosity. "If you would like, you can toss it a few meters and it will come right back to you."

"Ah ha," the mighty Jarl chortled, tossing it to his left; it missed a few of the gawking onlookers before it sprung back toward him like a tethered toy. There it hung, mere hairs away from the Jarl's face, its wings flapping. "Now that is truly remarkable, my man—what is your name?"

"I'm Am'ranth, my lord," he bowed. "They call me Am'ranth the Peddler around these parts, because of my trinkets."

"Trinkets? Ha!" The Krigan lord stood awestruck at the small toy in front of him. "This is quite remarkable. How did you make it do that? Is it the wings that are holding it up?"

"Oh no," he said. "You see, the wings are decorative, there is a small engine inside, much like what we use on our larger transports and spacecraft and it—"

"There is a bloody jet engine inside of this toy?" he asked. "Surely you jest."

"Oh no, my lord. I've come up with a way to build small engines that work proportionally with whatever they need to propel, from small toys such as these to larger things such as vehicles."

"Vehicles?"

"Yes," he said. "Actually, the transport I use has been modified with one of my engines and is quite efficient, much more so than any of the ones on the market right now."

"You are telling me that all of these companies and research firms in the capital, all the people working for me, and you, some Helgean monk, have found a better way?"

"Yes, well," he said, "I believe so. Although I could be wrong, my lord."

"I like this one," Quorthon said, turning back to his guards, who stood unamused. "Show me this transport of yours."

Quorthon was so impressed by how the transport functioned that he wasted no time and asked if Am'ranth could modify his own personal transports in his fleet with the same technology. The engine allowed them to hover higher than most of the transports available and used solar cells to keep a charge. Am'ranth had tried to explain the minutiae of the engine to him, but the Jarl seemed to care little about the details, just the result. All that mattered was that it was efficient and that it allowed for suborbital flight if needed, which for a man as powerful and visible as the Jarl of Krigar, could come in handy.

He loaded the last of the boxes onto his transport containing the parts he'd need to modify the five transports Quorthon had asked him to do. Am'ranth had tried to convince him to bring the crafts to his workshop in Cydonia, but his advisers had insisted that it be completed within the confines of the palace in the Krigan capital of Krigar, where they could monitor everything. There was no reason for the mighty Krigans, the seafaring pillagers of the planet Andlios, to fear the peaceful monks from Helgea, but the leader of the Krigan people had to be careful, they had explained.

The job became more difficult for Am'ranth considering the conditions, especially not knowing what type of facilities they would have at the palace. He did his best to remember everything, but there would surely be something he forgot and would need to borrow. While he understood that anything the Jarl of Krigar wished for he'd have, he still felt most comfortable with his own tools and his own workshop. He would have to make do, but he could feel the pressure building up in his chest and he understood what making the Jarl of Krigar happy could do for him.

A coughing fit overcame Am'ranth, and he did his best to mask it by coughing into an old rag that he kept handy for such occasions. The fits were growing in frequency and violence, but he knew that there wasn't much that could be done for him without more money. He glanced down at the rag, almost afraid of what he'd see. A man like him was smart, and he knew that the traces of blood had amplified in the last few weeks to where speckles became blots. He balled the rag back up, dutifully ignoring the spreading blood before stuffing it back into his pocket. If he made the Jarl happy his life could change in the blink of an eye, and he could beat back the Dreadlung yet.

THE ANDLIOSIAN COUNTRYSIDE was still a thing of beauty to Am'ranth after thirty-two cycles on the planet. Since his transport could fly high enough above the ground to not worry about damaging any of the flora and low enough to not register as a commercial flight, he could avoid the paved roads that connected all of Andliosian civilization together. He had traversed the road from Cydonia to Krigar many times in his life, but had never enjoyed it. It was the wet season, so while the weather was overcast and raining in most areas, the forests became lusher and fuller of life the closer he got to the great city of Krigar.

Cydonia existed to the North of Krigar, cradled in the heart of a mountain system, which meant that there was plant life there, but the rocky environment left things rather limited in their gradient, shifting from brown and gray to brown and green. Krigar, on the other hand, sat nestled on the outskirts of the Freyjan Forest, built right next to the ocean where the Krigan people felt connected to their seafaring roots. Am'ranth was a descendent from the people of the desert, the Zarr'nid people, although he had taken a vow when he was of age to join the Helgean Order and leave his old life behind.

His family had protested the decision, but Am'ranth had seen how his people were living and felt that there had to be more to life than living in the desert and scrounging for food and water while the rest of Andlios was living with the modern comforts. His faith in the Gods wasn't strong before, but joining the Helgean Order meant he could stay close to his Zarr'nid roots while still getting to experience more of the world than he would have tucked away in the vast deserts of Zariha to the east.

Now he was aboard his modified transport bounding over the rolling hills of the Krigan countryside inbound to Krigar, where he'd work personally on the Jarl of Krigar's fleet of transports. The excitement was palpable, and he finally felt like his decision to join the Order had been the right path for his life. In fact, Am'ranth had almost forgotten that he was a Helgean and that he had taken vows to the Order. This meant that while in Krigar he'd need to attend the daily services and stay in a monastery, which was an inconvenience, but a manageable one at least.

Before long, he merged back onto the main road leading into Krigar, marveling at how clean the architecture was by comparison. Though he had been there many times before, he had always been confined to the outskirts and it had always been on supply runs to the monasteries there. For the first time in his life, he could really see Krigar for what it was: amazing. While Cydonia was old, dusky, and decaying, Krigar always looked as if it had a fresh polish on it. Krigar was more ancient than Cydonia, but the care given to the city was immaculate. Appearances mattered. The great city was the perfect blend of tradition and technology and he was unable to contain the sheer awe while he approached the mighty iron gates to the palace. He had driven through the heart of the city, noticing for the first time how many residents were immaculately dressed in sharp, clean clothing that made his robe feel like rags in comparison. Everything about Krigar felt alive, while Cydonia felt like a place where ideas went to die in the old ways. They were waiting for him and he was pointed toward a small garage, where he pulled in and found the Jarl waiting for him. A wry smile adorned his face.

"Am'ranth, my friend." The Jarl approached, his mighty arms outstretched. Am'ranth jumped from the transport and sheepishly reached his hand out, Quorthon violently gripping onto his forearm with his large hand, which he haphazardly returned.

"Jarl Quorthon. I've brought everything I need with me to modify your vehicles; where should I set up shop?"

"I'm having my men bring the transports into the garage at once, we'll ensure that you have everything you need in due time, my friend. If you wouldn't mind indulging me, would you care for a tour of the palace?"

"Of course."

The invitation was unexpected, to say the least. Being a man of limited means and of the old Gods, he had expected to be ushered to the workspace tucked away deep in the bowels of the imposing palace, not being given a tour by the Jarl himself. History had taught him to temper his expectations and be mindful of what his place was in the world. This was the kind of shame that he knew growing up in the desert, disinterested with the old way of life and everything that came along with it. Everything about this trip felt alien to him, although he was grateful for the new experience.

Quorthon led him through the palace, listlessly and mechanically describing the wealth and power that came with the title of Jarl of Krigar. The palace had been constructed with care, built with marble floors and rustic wooden walls to emulate the style of the old longhouses that the original Jarls of Krigar had inhabited many cycles prior, but Quorthon languished inside those grand halls. They finally stopped inside a large wooden room that had been built to look like an ancient Great Hall, Quorthon opting to sit in a random seat at the table as opposed to on the dais and atop the throne. He swept his hand out, inviting Am'ranth to take a seat across the table from him.

"This is quite a place," Am'ranth said, his eyes scanning the great room, the sun streaming in through the windows near the seam where the walls met the pitched ceiling. The table had an ornate wave pattern carved with care into it, and the dark leather-lined chair looked immaculate.

"I agree," the Jarl said. "In fact, I had this specifically built into the palace. Nothing else quite felt like home. There is the throne room, of course, and many other rooms to receive in, but this one is something my forefathers would be proud of. You are Zarr'nid, correct?"

"Yes, my lord."

"Oh come now," he said, pounding his meaty fists on the ornate wooden table. "It is just the two of us here. Damn the formalities."

"Of course," Am'ranth said, apprehensive to drop the formalities. The Jarl was kind, but his temper was legendary and he could only imagine what it would be like to be around him if he was truly upset.

"The engines you brought were mostly intact, correct?"

"Mostly, yes, although they need some assembly," he said. "Why do you ask?"

"Don't be upset, but right now my men are studying your transport and working on installing your engines into the fleet without you. It's nothing personal. I am just surrounded by some of the most intelligent men on this planet and they are fully capable of a simple installation job."

"I see," he said, uneasy at the development. The excitement he had held melted, giving way to uncertainty of what his purpose was if all they wanted were the engines. "If you don't mind me saying, my lord, but I could have simply had the engines shipped if that were the case."

"That you could. Am'ranth, I didn't ask you here to install the engines aboard my fleet—although that is certainly still happening and you will be fully compensated for them and the labor that you would have spent—but I wanted you here for something else."

"Oh?"

"Yes. You see, I'm the Jarl of Krigar, one in a long line of Jarls that will go down in the Great Book without much to celebrate or to live on forever. There are no great wars on the horizon, no heroic battles, invaders, or raiding anymore. Instead, this is all so..." He twirled his finger in the air. "Unremarkable?"

"I disagree," Am'ranth said. "You are one of the most powerful men in all of Andlios, you'll never want for anything again, nor should you. There are many living without these luxuries, no offense."

"None taken," he let out a laugh. "See, this is what I had hoped for: an honest man willing to speak his mind with me and not be so scared all the time. Everyone nods and agrees with me; they hang off my every word, but these are not remarkable times, my friend."

"I'm not sure how I can help with that," Am'ranth said, unable to determine the great Jarl's intent. "I'm not a remarkable man myself."

"That is where we must disagree. I'm not looking to start a war or dash out into the expanse anytime soon. I'm simply looking to be remembered. I wish to create a symbol for Krigan power that will live on for generations."

"You mean like a logo or a crest?" He felt a coughing fit starting to erupt and he scrambled into his pocket to produce his handkerchief.

"That cough there sounds serious," the Jarl noted, stroking

the length of his flowing blonde beard. "But no, not quite. I'm looking for a weapon, one that would demonstrate Krigan power and tradition but would be a bit more eloquent. Right now, everything is crude blasters and axes, both the long great axes and the single-handed ones. Most consider the ax to be a clumsy, dated weapon, but truth be told, in tight quarters there are not as many weapons that can be as graceful and brutal as the ax."

"I see," Am'ranth said, quietly pocketing his handkerchief without inspecting it for blood, pushing the lingering doubts of his illness out of his mind.

"Look." He unstrapped the ornately carved great ax from his back, slamming it down on the table between them, sinking the etched blade into the soft wood. "It is a beautiful weapon, but we as a people are moving toward more small arms—blasters, rifles, and the like. If we could somehow combine the two eloquently into one weapon, then it would be something I'd be remembered for."

"I think I see what you are saying," he said. "You want an ax that doubles as a blaster or a rifle."

"Exactly!" His fist pounded down on the table, the ax remaining embedded firmly. "I've had teams working up prototypes and none of them are satisfactory. They are clumsy; they look like a blaster attached to the end of an ax. I want integration, but they claim it is not possible without sacrificing power. This is where you come into the equation."

"While I appreciate the thought." Am'ranth tried to force a smile, but his mind was racing at the seemingly impossible task. "But I've never dealt with weaponry before, being a Helgean monk and all. My Lord, this is a simple task fit more for those familiar with war and weaponry."

"You underestimate yourself, Am'ranth. I have the finest minds in the Krigan empire working night and day for the betterment of all humanity, yet you, a simple monk living in Cydonia, came up with an efficient, compact propulsion engine that is scalable. I don't think you understand, my friend, that alone could have altered the course of history. We can utilize your technology to revolutionize everything. Even space travel will be easier with the new Am'ranth Engine."

"My gods," he muttered, marveling at hearing the name out loud. "You aren't serious, are you?"

"Of course I am. I'm the damned Jarl of Krigar. Your technology is beyond what I've ever seen. Building some silly weapon should not be out of your reach."

"I guess I could try, I just..." He felt lost, like a child, as lost as the day he had left his family and the caravan to become a Helgean monk. "I wasn't prepared for this at all."

"But you can build it?"

"I think I can, yes."

"Good!"

TWO

THE PULSEAXE

uilding a prototype for a weapon was a lot more complicated than Am'ranth was prepared for. Matters weren't helped with Quorthon being a perfectionist with the weapon they had been calling the "pulseaxe." He felt it was his legacy, what he would be remembered for, and the symbol for Krigan power and ingenuity. Krigan culture was built on the tenets of strength, valor, and domination, with some justice and honor mixed in for good measure. Nothing said strength to them like their traditional weaponry.

In Quorthon's view, building a weapon that would stand the test of time, blending the old with the new and allowing for their traditional axes to live on as a new form of weapon, was what would cement him a place in history. The whole idea seemed silly and petty to Am'ranth, who grew up in a caravan, where their only possessions were what they could pack onto a mule or a horse. They didn't have the luxury of splendid halls, instead living in tent cities they would construct when it grew cold and tear down when they needed to move to a different part of the desert. Being a Helgean monk was also a life where belongings were few and far between, with each Helgean taking an oath of poverty for the betterment of everyone around them and to serve the Gods.

Life for the Helgeans was dedicated to spreading the word of the Gods, the Elder Ones of yore. They served no political purpose, had no armies or weapons, and their history was one of service to the Gods. The longer he spent working on the pulseaxe, the more often he had forgotten about the Gods entirely, missing the daily prayers and instead focusing on his creation. To make matters worse, his coughing fits had intensified, which had forced him to go to a doctor, and the prognosis was grim. The doctor had confirmed what he already knew: that he was suffering from the Dreadlung, which if they had caught earlier on they would have been able to treat, but since it had advanced for so long because of his inherent stubbornness, it had spread to the point of almost entirely consuming his left lung. Sometimes he paid it no mind, while other times he fought for each breath. They had given him medications and painkillers, which helped but a painful death loomed heavy on the horizon, a veritable albatross tied around his neck.

He did his best to not bother Quorthon with his health woes, especially considering that his temper was growing shorter and shorter with each passing day. Am'ranth's focus grew scattered as well, and he spent considerable time researching artificial lungs as opposed to the inner workings of blasters. Breathing apparatus like this was not yet a technology that existed in any true manner. While there were machines that could pump oxygen into a lung in the hospital, they were a life-saving measure, though—a stopgap, not a permanent solution.

The notoriety that had come with the advent of the

Am'ranth Engine becoming one of the latest advances in technology meant that his humble workshop in the palace's basement had grown to suit the scope of his new project, which was to achieve immortality for Jarl Quorthon. Since Am'ranth was Helgean and did his best to honor his vows—even if he had stopped praying or believing—he donated the patent for the engine and made it publicly available, allowing for any and all companies to use the technology without restrictions.

There were considerable measured responses to such an act. Many of the transport companies were embarrassed that someone who had tinkered in a workshop with limited means had outdone all of their cycles and gold crowns they had spent on research. Some were outraged and believed it to be a fabrication, while many celebrated this mysterious figure who came from obscurity and brought such an amazing technological leap with him—and even better, distributing it for free. He was so lost in thought that he almost didn't hear the sound of the door to his workshop squeak open, but he snapped out of his reverie and turned around to see Quorthon stalking into the room.

"Shit, I almost didn't hear you," Am'ranth said, having dropped the formalities long ago.

"Is there any progress, Am'ranth? I am a patient man, you know this, but this project should have been completed many fortnights ago." The Jarl walked up to the workbench, snatching up a prototype for a synthetic lung, inspecting it and dropping it back down onto the table. "While I appreciate your health concerns and your side projects, we had agreed upon delivering the pulseaxe by now."

"There wasn't a specific time frame given, you and I both know that," he said, walking over to one of his workbenches where the latest prototypes sat. "But I think these new proto-types might be to your liking."

"Hopefully better than the last set," he said, Am'ranth noting hints of annoyance in his tone.

"I'd like to think so." Am'ranth picked up a smaller ax from the table, one that would fit in a hand, and held it out toward the Jarl. "I believe that the form factor should be right this time, and I was able to overcome the heat sink issues we've been having whenever the blaster mechanism is shrunk down to this size."

"Without a loss in power or range like before?" the Jarl asked, snatching the blaster up to inspect it.

"This one should be just as powerful as the standard sidearm that your men carry," he said, taking a certain pride in his work. "But is also an ax. The ax is quite balanced, you'll find."

"It feels good." He took a few swipes at the air with it. "Good heft, too. Let me see how this fires." He turned it around, holding onto the base of the blade where the grip was, aiming at the wall and pulling the trigger. A flash of light erupted from the weapon and a slight pulsing sound filled the air before they both looked at the wall and saw a hole punched in it the size of a man's fist. "My gods, Am'ranth." He let out a laugh and turned, beaming. "I think we've done it!"

"Thank the Gods." He felt relieved, able to take pride in his work. "Now for the bigger model, it has a much longer range and more power; I'm not sure you want to be aiming it at the wall or—"

"Oh please," Quorthon scoffed. "These walls are replace-able, but our place in history? My friend, they'll be drinking to us in the hall up high for this. Why don't you try that one, bask in the glory of it, my friend?"

"Okay." He picked up the larger ax and held it like a rifle, pressing the base of the top of the blade up against his shoulder where he had installed a padded surface that wouldn't impact any of the cutting ability. He pointed the barrel at the wall right next to the hole that Quorthon had just blown, smiled, and pulled the trigger. The heat was almost overbearing. In the matter of a heartbeat, it was clear that something was wrong. He was shot back a few meters while everything burned, everything turned black, and the world buzzed.

WARM SUNLIGHT STREAMED in from the windows of the strange room, giving it an otherworldly feeling. Stark white curtains were the first thing Am'ranth saw when he opened his left eye. Everything was a blur, the fog only beginning to lift when he realized where he was. There were monitors all over the room and tubes running between his body and some of the equipment that surrounded him. Fear bubbled up inside him while he regained control of his senses, realizing that he couldn't see out of his right eye and that most of his right side felt numb. Am'ranth let out a muffled scream, only for the door to open and a team of men entered the room.

"What...is...happening?" he mumbled, pain shooting through his jaw.

"He's awake," one man said, studying the readout. "Go find the Jarl."

A second man dashed out of the room while the first continued studying the instruments that encircled his bed. The room seemed like it was closing in around him. His inability to control parts of himself only intensified the terror. His mind raced back to his last memories, of being in the workshop with Quorthon and the rifle exploding in his hands. Am'ranth's time had an expiration date already, never mind accounting for a rifle exploding in his hands.

"Tell...me..." Speaking burned his throat and made his jaw ache. There were layers of gauze wrapped all over his body, making it confusing as to what was difficult to move because of the gauze and what was because of the injuries.

"Jarl Quorthon will be here shortly," the man said before walking out of the room, leaving Am'ranth alone inside the circle of instruments.

"Tell...me..."

"My friend," Quorthon's voice boomed as he entered the room. Am'ranth strained to turn his head but found his neck set in place, and the left side of the room was obscured because of the patch over his eye. "I heard you were awake."

"What...the..."

"Don't talk." Quorthon moved around the bed, sitting down on a chair by the window on the right side, where Am'ranth could see him. "Quite a scare there, I must say. I walked away with a few burns, but things weren't as simple for you, my friend. My medical team has been tending to your needs day and night and they tell me you'll live, but, things won't be quite the same. Mind you, I should note that your case of the Dreadlung is much worse than you had let on, so much of this won't matter for long."

There was an awkward pause, Am'ranth mulling over what he had already known about his Dreadlung and mortality and his newfound injuries. It was what he had suspected from the moment he awoke, but hearing it out loud made it much more real. The rest of his life was already going to be uncomfortable, as he was already struggling to breathe. Now it would involve portions of his body not cooperating at all.

"The good news," Quorthon smiled at him, "is that we found the malfunction in the prototype and have corrected it. So we've done it, my friend, we've built the pulseaxe! History will remember us as heroes, my friend."

THREE

FORGE THE FUTURE

Am'ranth's workshop in Cydonia remained unchanged, yet his outlook was grim. The workshop was still a small building with a tin roof, but the idea of meddling with trinkets, propulsion engines, or even what he had worked on in the depths of the palace in Krigar seemed trivial in the face of certain impending death. Instead, survival would need to line the walls of his workshop. The development of an artificial lung was his first trial and perhaps the most difficult. The tests he ran on his prototypes all resulted in what would cause life-threatening infections if installed in his chest.

Without a filter, the air intake would only be functional for mere months. He would require the removal of possibly both lungs to install the new ones, which would be tasked to one of the local doctors he trusted. There was a small community of enthusiasts in Cydonia that Am'ranth had aligned himself with since he had limped back home from Krigar. Initially, he felt it would be a heroic homecoming, but instead he had slinked home and neglected his duties to the Helgean Order. As far as he was concerned, he was no longer a brother of the Order; he was just a broken soul engaged in a desperate search for a way to cling onto life for however long he could.

"Am'ranth." The young Piotr bound into the room. His energy was both infectious and obnoxious, depending on the mood that Am'ranth found himself in. The boy was Zarr'nid, much like himself, and was obsessed with trying to wrap his head around everything Am'ranth did. Am'ranth was a hero to the boy, even in his embittered, broken state that kept him away from mirrors or much self-reflection.

"Yes," he said, still unadjusted to the whirring, sing-song hum of his voice. He had developed a device that could project his voice further and clean up the audio, but wearing it around his neck grew cumbersome with each passing day.

"Dr. Zun'thir is here to see you."

"Send her in," he said, still fixated on the lung.

"Mr. El Siddig." The lithe doctor walked in, wearing a warm smile on her face. Her dark hair was pulled back into a tight ponytail and her sullen expression was professional, if not serious. She outstretched her hand, only to rescind the gesture at Am'ranth's lack of interest. "So how has the research been going?"

"Fine. The only answer I have for the filter is to wear a special respirator, though."

"From the data I've seen that would be the only way, I agree." The doctor pulled up a rolling stool to sit on. "It might not be the best way, but for right now it seems to be the only way outside of surgery every few months, which could be an option, but your body will only be able to handle so much and infections are bound to happen."

"I've developed a special helmet." He pushed around the debris on his desk, uncovering the sketched blueprints for the helmet, handing it over to the doctor, who studied it. "The respirator should suffice, the visor would include a display of my vital signs and allow for me to always be monitoring my statistics, plus..." Am'ranth pulled the amplifier closer to his mouth, twisting a knob and noticing the difference. "...It might force me to use this more, make it easier for people to understand me."

"It would have to be a lifelong commitment." The doctor set the plans back down onto the table. "You'd have to come up with a plan for feeding, as well, because this helmet would be your connection to life if you opted for it. At least until we found a better way."

"Who knows? I might even grow to enjoy having a display of everything around me and use it even if I don't need it."

"See," the doctor smiled at him, "that's the spirit right there."

"Doctor." He tugged the amplifier aside, speaking in his gurgling, raspy voice. "Have you inspected the robotics I asked you to?"

"Then there is that," the doctor said. "Look, Am'ranth, I looked over the prototypes and I can't advise it. I know you had your hopes pinned on it and helped Davoth develop them, but we don't know if they'll be stable. It would require neural mapping, which is simply beyond my comprehension, plus, well, it would take humanity into a dangerous direction."

"I've developed weapons, engines for warships, and now artificial lungs to keep me alive." He chose his words with great care. "If these robotics—these augmentations—could help people, genuinely help people, I'm willing to be the test subject. Trust me, I'm already dead a few times over, Dr. Zun'thir."

"I'll do it," the doctor let a resigned sigh escape, "but don't expect me to be happy with it and if anything goes wrong—

and I mean anything—I will abort the operation. All of this is very unusual and I can't assure you that you'll be much better off."

"Doctor, I have a useless right arm, a barely functional right leg, and half of my face shows no movement or emotion. I'm already a monster in the eyes of most, but if just my arm could be useful again it would all be worth it, I could work on building again without needing everyone else to help with my prototypes."

"Am'ranth, nobody minds helping you. You are a visionary, you are one of our great minds. If you want my advice, stop feeling sorry for yourself. You've done amazing things already, immortality is already within your reach."

"Thank you, doctor, but I didn't ask for advice. I ask that you perform the procedures as directed."

"Oh, I didn't mean to offend you, Am'ranth," the doctor said, carefully picking her words. "But as a professional, your health and well-being come first. These inventions may be your own, but I'll be the woman cutting into and placing these... these...augmentations, as you called them, into a local legend. There's some pressure involved in all of this."

"I understand. You install the augmentations and that will be all, I'm more than capable of fine-tuning them on my own."

FOR THE SECOND TIME, Am'ranth woke up in a hospital bed, this one less serene and clean than the room inside the palace in Krigar. His throat burned, and he wore a makeshift respirator over his face, still with no feeling in his right arm, and a dull throbbing in his leg. The doctor sat in the corner, staring out the window, the sharp features on her face wracked with concern.

"Doctor," Am'ranth said, hearing his voice coming from the amplification unit on the respirator.

"You're awake." She stood up, forcing an apprehensive smile. "The surgeries were a success. It was a long day and there were a few tense moments, but I installed everything according to the plans Davoth provided to me. As for functionality, I'm not sure. I'm not equipped for such things."

"That's fine," he said, trying to will himself to move his arm to no avail. "When can I leave?"

"Leave? You just came to, we'll want to keep you for observation for at least a few days."

"Is Davoth here now?"

"Yes, he's just right outside, but I'd recommend—"

"Send him in," he interrupted, feeling agitated by the doctor. It wasn't her fault, but Am'ranth had his own equipment to monitor the augmentations and make any changes that he saw fit.

"Alright, but if something goes wrong, I'll be right outside."

"Thank you, Doctor."

The doctor exited the room and Am'ranth took a deep breath. What struck him was how easy it was to breathe again. He would have to adjust to life with the respirator on his face, but it wasn't all that uncomfortable compared to how difficult it was to fight for every breath like he had to before. The arm was dead weight—heavy dead weight at that—but there were ways beyond complicated neural programming to make such a part function.

A brooding man entered the room, heavyset with untamed, curly gray-and-brown hair and a large beard, carrying a sack slung over his shoulder. "So I heard it went well," Davoth said, setting the bag down on the table next to the bed.

"Yes, the augmentations are all in, but of course not functional yet."

"Of course not," the large man's face lit up, pulling out a helmet from the bag. "You don't have this yet."

"Have you been testing it?"

"It isn't without its bugs yet, but the computer we installed can receive commands from the neural scanner. We'll have to find a way for the electrodes to be a bit less intrusive, it's still a work in progress..."

"Did it control the bionics, Davoth?"

"I don't want to get your hopes up, Am'ranth," he said, sitting down on the bed and holding the helmet in his lap. "But yes, it did. This was with my mind, though, but it worked."

"My Gods," he muttered, Davoth ambling over toward the top of the bed.

"Alright, I'm going to connect these electrodes to the ports we had the doctor install. I have no clue how it is going to feel, to be honest, since I was using simple contact nodes before, and these are connected to your mind, operating as a synapse and... well shit, let's just give it a shot, alright?"

"Do it," he commanded, feeling Davoth's fingers on his forehead while the helmet sat beside his head. At first, it was just a click he felt, then a second, then a third, and fourth, each one forcing an alien vibration inside his head. Davoth carefully lifted the helmet up, tucking the wires inside the helmet, making sure they weren't getting in the way of anything. Am'ranth undid the respirator he was wearing and he held his breath while Davoth lowered the helmet the rest of the way.

Am'ranth picked his head up so that the helmet could be

secured, and Davoth snapped it shut and he took a deep, desperate breath while the respirator began pumping air.

"How does it feel?" Davoth asked.

"Strange," he said, a readout of his blood pressure, heart rate, and other vital statistics blinking to life on the screen. "Respirator is functional, readouts are good."

"Okay, now time to test the arm and leg out." Davoth licked his lips, standing back from the bed. "Just...you know, think about moving a finger. Focus."

"Alright," he said, imagining moving his right finger. He turned and looked down, seeing the robotic hand unflinching. "Damnit."

"Keep trying. It takes a while to catch on, but once it does, my gods, it just works. Trust me."

"I knew I should have tested it further."

"Just keep trying. Focus Am'ranth, believe in our work."

"Fine." He looked down at the unflinching hand, closing his eye and focusing on just the arm, just the hand, just the finger. He focused on just the finger and how it would feel to move the finger. He tried to shut out any other thoughts, just the finger.

"The Gods!" Davoth shouted. "The Gods!"

Am'ranth opened his eye and looked down at his mechanical hand, almost unable to believe the sight of the index finger curling and uncurling at his command. "It's working," he whispered. "It's working."

"You're damned right that it's working!" Davoth could barely contain his excitement. "Go on, try the rest. It's a cascade from there, just..."

The hand shot up, palm urging Davoth to quiet down. A surge of energy flowed through Am'ranth, the readout on his helmet noting the surge in heart rate. He curled the hand up into a fist and he couldn't help but let out a laugh at the sight of it. There was no feeling, but there was an odd, inexplicable connection he had with the hand. The hand reached out and pulled the sheet off him roughly, revealing the mechanical foot and shin woven into what remained of the living tissue of his leg, meaning the rest had been removed during the operation.

Feeling more confident now, he focused on the toe, gazing at it until it jumped. One after another the toes moved, the ankle moved, and he could bend and unbend the knee. The focus required to handle all of this would be difficult, but he'd learn how to control it in time. Limb independence felt like a miracle, something that humans had mastered for ages with little thought, but Am'ranth found himself having to devote an intense focus on moving either right limb.

"Slow down, Am'ranth," Davoth said. "You don't have to master it in one day, this will take weeks, months, cycles even to..."

Am'ranth slung both legs over the side of the bed, ripping his arms free from the IV lines that felt like relics of a past he had left behind, pulling the nodes off from his chest. He was still clumsy, and was forced to focus hard. With a great surge of energy, he pushed himself forward off the bed, landing on his left leg, the right one smashing into the ground with a crash and his body lurching forward toward the window. His right arm sprang out, catching onto the windowsill and keeping him standing.

"Slow down, damnit," Davoth cursed. "You don't need to push this hard, Am'ranth."

"I'll push as hard as I please," he said, straightening himself up only to feel like he was about to tip over again, but focused his mind on his right foot and stayed standing. With a pained thought, he put his left foot out in front of him, mustering up the strength to move the right one forward. It clunked forward, and he almost tipped again, but it was feeling more natural. Davoth was backing up toward the door, his jaw open in disbelief. Am'ranth took another step, more confident this time, then another.

"The gods," Davoth repeated. "You are doing it."

"Yes," he said, holding his right hand up and clenching his fist. "Davoth," he turned to his friend, "do you understand what we've accomplished today?"

"What?"

"This," he held his hand out. "This is the greatest achievement in human history. With this, we can become immortal."

FOUR

THE CYMAGE

Am'ranth stood in front of the mirror, wearing just a pair of underwear and his helmet. The man who once existed was no longer there; instead, the figure staring back at him was still very much human, but the machine parts were undeniable. The complex computer inside his helmet helped him understand both himself and the world around him better. It also controlled almost half of his body at this point.

Whenever he went out into public now, he wore a full body-suit, covering up his augmentations to avoid any further ridicule. The response to his surgeries was mixed: some in awe of what he had accomplished, seeing the scientific advances that came from it, the sacrifices he had made and the practical applications, while others saw him as a freak, a machine fetishist living in a world that didn't quite reject technology, but saw a blurred line, most convinced that he had crossed whatever boundary there was left to cross.

The man who ran the booth in Cydonia Square peddling his wares was no longer Am'ranth the Peddler, but now

Am'ranth the Cymage—a word amalgamated from Cydonia and the concept of him utilizing dark magic to prolong his life. They didn't understand, he had convinced himself. Even then, there was a growing number of supporters to his cause, those who had life-threatening or debilitating injuries and ailments of their own who had turned to Am'ranth for a solution, believing him to be working miracles.

Clearly he had stumbled onto something, a fountain of youth that came at the price of one's apparent humanity—at least to some. They had debates, some in public, mostly in private, and Am'ranth's loyal friends were always there to report back to him on where public opinion stood. The man who was once a powerless monk of the Helgean Order was now powerful, commanding a presence and had become a larger-than-life public figure. There was a growing number of people who turned to him for guidance and his public presence had to morph, much like his body had morphed over the previous few months.

He pulled on the full bodysuit he had custom built for himself. There were tiny electrodes all throughout that acted as receptors, delivering information to the main processor unit in his helmet, acting as sensory information for his augmented limbs. The suit was a part of a whole organism now that redefined his existence. He wore a black jacket over it, along with a pair of gloves and a crimson-red cape that draped over his shoulders. If they wanted him to be larger than life, then he would be what they imagined him to be.

Am'ranth stomped out the door of his room into the workshop, where a group was working on new prototypes, always looking to improve on what they'd already been building. "How are things going?"

"Not bad." Davoth turned on his stool to face him. "Dr. Zun'thir is performing two new augmentation surgeries tomorrow."

"Excellent," he said, pacing around the room.

"Interestingly enough, both have requested helmets much like yours."

"Like mine? Do they have respiratory issues?"

"No, not quite," he said. "One has a problem with his heart and the other had an arm cleaved off by one of the Krigans a while back."

"So they want helmets to what, control and monitor?"

"I think they just look up to you, Am'ranth."

"Their faces aren't mangled like mine, I presume, not forced to live life breathing and eating through a tube, so why?"

"Because you are special, Am'ranth, don't you get that already? These people look up to you, they want to be like you. You are a hero to them. These are people who were told that there was no hope and now they see hope in what we are doing here."

"It was never my intention, you know that."

"You said you wanted to change the world for the better. I'd say we have."

"I guess so," he said, overwhelmed by the prospect of actually making an even deeper impact on human culture. "I think I'll go for a walk, maybe head over to the hospital and check in on Dr. Zun'thir."

"That's great," Davoth said, "but you don't have to, really, I sent Piotr there to help them along when they come to."

"Piotr? He's just a boy."

"You're correct, he might be, but at the same time, he's the most astute of the bunch and has gleaned much from both of us. He handled the last three weeks without incident."

"Fair enough. I still would like to be there and see the process for myself."

The westward wind made for a brisk afternoon. Not that those sensations were of his concern anymore, the readouts from his display told him all he needed to know about the world around him. He didn't need to feel it himself to understand what was happening, not anymore. The wind in Cydonia was overwhelming most afternoons, cascading down off the mountains and sweeping through the Cydonian valley. He thought back to his youth and how he'd fly kites in the wind or how he helped develop his Am'ranth Engine in that very wind. Inspiration found him in different ways, like the wind taking a feather and pushing it further than it could ever travel on its own.

Now it all seemed so inconsequential, crushed under a sea of raw, comprehensive data. The tactile world was slipping from his grasp, which at first had concerned him, but he processed data at unfathomable rates, integrating his own thoughts and movements in with his computer so quickly that his concerns melted away. Since he had awoken from his surgery he had been steadily upgrading that computer and the capability of his sensors and suit; he'd never be satisfied until he achieved perfection. It was far from perfect now, but he could tend to most of his daily functions without interruption or hiccup, which was vital considering the sheer amount of technology that sat nestled in his body.

"You fucking freak," a voice rang out from behind him. He sensed an incoming object, forcing him to act fast and dodge the projectile, and a bottle crashed down onto the pavement in front of him.

Am'ranth glared over at the man, a Krigan who was cursing at him and appeared to be heavily inebriated. "You seemed to have dropped something," he hissed at the man without a hint of irony.

"You are a fucking freak, I said." The man moved closer, an imposing man just over two meters tall with bulging muscles. "What you've done is unnatural, and now even more freaks are doing it. The Gods never intended for this."

"The Gods are inconsequential," Am'ranth said. "What I've done is help people, to help push humanity forward."

"Forward to what? Damnation?"

"No," he said. "Forward to controlling our own destiny, to being in command of life."

"I bet you think this is funny." The man placed his hands on Am'ranth's shoulders, grasping onto his cape. "Really fucking funny, isn't it?"

"I'd recommend you take your hands off of me."

"Or what?" The man gave him a shove, but he planted his right foot behind him, digging it into the trampled sand.

"Or this." In one fell swoop he sprang forward, his right shoulder smashing into the brick wall that was the man's body. The movement forced him to cock back and throw his fist, and it connected with the man's jaw, sending him crashing into the chair the man had been previously sitting in, groaning in a heap.

The man was out, but Am'ranth was not completely unharmed himself. It was the first truly physical act he had done since having the arm installed, and his shoulder felt extremely sore. He made a mental note that he'd need to have it looked into and possibly modified a bit more intensely to avoid such pains in the future. Without looking back, he continued down the road toward the hospital. There had been expectations of potential violence considering how many viewed augmenting man with machine parts as sacrilege, but soon they would understand once more had undergone surgeries and come out the better for it.

Am'ranth was stewing over the assault and conflicted about even bothering with visiting the hospital. The doctor could take care of things on her own, as she had been doing since his surgery. He was a well-respected member of Cydonian society, but it was clear that he would never receive the level of respect he deserved as long as he remained silent. At the next street, he made a left turn, heading back toward his workshop while running an internal diagnostic on his shoulder. It would be fine, the readout said, just recommending ice and rest. Rest would be difficult considering how quickly his mind was racing.

When he arrived at his ever-expanding workshop, he threw the door open only to find Davoth and the crew working. Davoth turned toward him with a grave expression on his face. "What happened to the hospital?"

"I was assaulted," he said, walking into the room massaging his shoulder.

"Gods, do we need to fix anything, are you alright?" Davoth hopped off the stool and was coming toward him, only for Am'ranth to motion him away.

"I'm fine," he said. "My shoulder is sore, but it will be fine. A man assaulted me in the streets, though, calling me a monster. Every day we operate in silence, in the shadows, people will learn to fear us. They won't know that we are here to help them, to help humanity. Do we have the equipment to record a video and to broadcast it?"

"Recording is no problem," Davoth said. "As for broadcasting, we don't have the means."

"Mr. Am'ranth, sir," one assistant raised his hand.

"Yes?" He turned toward the boy, no older than 17 but already one of his converts, wearing a mechanical bracer on his left arm and a specially constructed band on his head to help control it.

"My brother works at the Cydonian Outpost."

"Interesting." He crossed his arms. "The news station?"

"Yes," he said. "I could convince him to place it on the news, especially after what you did for me. My entire family is indebted to you."

"Consider there no debt. Deliver this and we'll never ask for more from you."

"Thank you, sir." The boy hopped up, dashing into the next room.

"Davoth." He turned to his friend. "Set up the equipment."

"LADIES AND GENTLEMEN OF ANDLIOS." They stood huddled over the screen in the workshop around Am'ranth, watching his recording from earlier airing on the news station that was broadcasting to Cydonia and the neighboring areas. "My name is Am'ranth El Siddig, better known to my friends in Cydonia as Am'ranth the Peddler or, of late, Am'ranth the Cymage by detractors. If you are unaware, I began as a poor boy of a caravan before entering the Helgean Order. I showed an aptitude for what many called tinkering.

"That tinkering led to the development of what is now known as the Am'ranth Engine, which many have heralded as one of the greatest advances in propulsion in our history." The image of Am'ranth on the screen was unwavering, his suit projecting strength beyond his wildest imagination. "Then, in a partnership with the Jarl of Krigar, I helped build the pulseaxe, a modern weapon for a peaceful time. During the development of that weapon, there was an accident, and I found myself not only a man dying of the Dreadlung, but also a man mangled by an explosion.

"Survival became an obsession, which led to the development of an intricate artificial lung system that was surgically installed into my body along with a few other state-of-the-art modifications." He held his right hand out toward the screen, removing his glove with his left hand, unveiling his mechanical hand. The camera focused on the hand, the fingers moving naturally while the mechanisms were plain for all to see in motion. "This has included one of the greatest advances in medical technology that our people could ever imagine; this hand is a symbol for all that could be.

"Through technology, I can live a fruitful life again in complete control of a body that once broke down on me. I will no longer die of the Dreadlung and my injuries will hinder me no longer. This is not about me, though, this is about the men and women who have opted to undergo procedures right here in Cydonia, through Dr. Zun'thir with my personal guidance. From replacement organs to temporary and permanent limb replacements, we have been able to provide hope to the hopeless, to enter a new age for humanity.

"Some have dubbed me a monster, have claimed that I have forgotten the Gods and forged my own path, creating myself in the image of a god. That is patently false. Instead, what I've done is sacrificed my body for the future of humanity and while nothing is perfect, I have given hope to many and will continue to do so. I've heard the snickering on the streets, the words bandied about. 'Cymage' they call me as if there is trickery or black magic involved. I assure you that it is science, and that there is nothing to fear outside of the survival and evolution of our people."

The interview ended, and the room remained silent while the newscaster appeared on the screen to continue the program. Davoth flicked the screen off and turned back toward Am'ranth, eyes red and tears welling up. "My gods." He held his arms out, Am'ranth quickly accepting the embrace. "It was beautiful, my friend. Just beautiful. We are doing something wonderful here."

"I agree." Am'ranth felt the emotions stirring inside him only to suppress them with a dark coldness from deep inside. He appreciated his friend's support but saw the road ahead and how rough it would be. "Going public was the only option at this point. The road ahead will not be easy, my friends." The men stopped their embrace, and Am'ranth turned toward the rest in the workshop. "From here on out we will be reviled, feared, and deified for what we are doing. If you cannot handle this, then the door is right there." He pointed at the workshop's door. "But know this—we are helping people and the people of Andlios can only benefit from what we have to do and no one will stop us. No one," he reiterated.

FIVE

OLD FRIENDS

Am'ranth stood in the marble and wooden hallway of the palace in Krigar with his hands clenched behind his back, patiently awaiting his audience with the Jarl of Krigar. He had requested an official audience, and Quorthon had immediately accepted it through an intermediary. There was a seeming lack of sincerity by Quorthon not extending the invitation on his own, but Am'ranth knew political matters had become difficult since his broadcast and the growing number of people in Cydonia opting for augmentations.

He stood admiring a painting of Quorthon at the end of the hall. The portrait was of Quorthon standing heroically on a shore, a wolf pelt wrapped over his broad shoulders and an ornate pulseaxe in his hand. The irony of the situation was not lost on Am'ranth as he heard the door open, a smaller, plainly dressed man stepping out. "Mr. El Siddig, he'll see you now."

"Thank you," he said, stepping through the mighty doors to the audience chamber. He wasn't being received in Quorthon's Great Hall, which was an omen of discomfort at this visit;

instead, Quorthon opted for the more formal throne room meant for official business.

"My old friend." Quorthon stood on the dais, stepping down and extending his hand.

"My lord." He gripped onto Quorthon's forearm, Quorthon returning the gesture but Am'ranth only receiving minor tactile information from the interaction. Much had changed since their last meeting, with the scales of power shifting ever-so-slightly in Am'ranth's favor, to the extent where his grip was far stronger than the hulking Krigan's.

"That is quite a grip you have there," he said. "Last I remembered, that hand wasn't good for much."

"A lot has changed since then."

"I've gathered as much." He looked behind and stepped back onto the dais, sitting back into his throne. "I've seen your public proclamation and heard the stories. To be certain, you have quite a following now, my old friend."

"Both of us know I never intended for that. You had shown me that I could change the world, so I've accepted my fate and do what I can."

"So you have." His expression changed. "But this isn't the Am'ranth Engine or the pulseaxe, my friend, this is different, very different."

"I'm not sure I follow."

"When I met you, Am'ranth, you were a man of the gods," he explained, Am'ranth's readouts showing him that the man was nervous. "You were a man of the cloth, even. If somehow I led you to believe that you should abandon that path...I am very sorry, but—"

"My former profession," he said, taking great care in choosing his words, "was simply that. You helped show me that

I could impact the lives of many, my lord, but my decision was my own. You remember how I was after that accident."

"Aye. You were dying. In fact, we thought you wouldn't last the cycle. Instead, here you are, some mangled man and machine hybrid, spitting in the face of the Gods!" His pulse was rising.

"I can feel the disgust from here. I regret coming here. It appears I've wasted both of our time on this."

"Do not just walk out like that, Am'ranth," he ordered. "You came here for a reason and knew what my reaction would be."

"I suppose I knew what would happen," he said. "Although I had hoped that our partnership in the past could extend into today. You should know that I am looking to extend my services beyond Cydonia, possibly even open a clinic here in Krigar."

"I must decline."

"This does not surprise me."

"My friend, it is not too late." It sounded like the mighty Quorthon was pleading. "You've strayed from the path and I know you were in pain, but where you are headed and pushing humanity is a dark place. You do not understand what you are advocating for."

"But I do. I've seen people in pain, people dying, much like myself. Instead of dying they can live on, their knowledge and experience continuing forward with them. The world is changing, Quorthon, the old ways are evolving, much like that pulseaxe I developed is the evolution of the old way."

"A bloody ax that fires a shot differs from man becoming a machine!" he barked.

"I'm just as human as I ever was," Am'ranth said. "In fact, I am just as human as you are."

"By the Gods."

"This has nothing to do with the Gods."

"That is where you are wrong, my friend," he spat spite and disgust with his words, "for I am the Mighty Quorthon, the Jarl of Krigar, leader of the Krigan people! The heart that beats in my chest is of my own, as is everything else. I was hand assembled and selected by the Gods to lead my people, and I refuse to let you bastardize that! Go." He motioned with disgust. "Get out of my sight before you anger me further. Leave me and leave my people alone. You are not to return to Krigar again."

"Quorthon..." Am'ranth felt as if someone had punched him in the stomach. He knew the Jarl wouldn't accept these changes without a discussion, but had hoped that the man who had called him a friend would see some of his old friend and listen. "Won't you listen to reason?"

"Reason?" He snatched up his pulseaxe from next to the throne and sprang to his feet. "This was reason! This was within nature! This was evolution! You? Ha, you are unnatural."

"You are making a mistake." He shook his head. "A grave mistake. You want to be remembered? What better way than the betterment of humanity; you don't want the history books to view you as the coward who was staring evolution in the eye only to cast it away because of ignorance."

"Ignorance? Ha!" Quorthon snapped, stepping down from the dais with the pulseaxe in hand. He pointed it at Am'ranth as he circled around him. "You know nothing of the sort. Your ignorance is on full display. You wish to become a god and I will not facilitate this. I am not the fool you take me to be and you are no friend of mine."

"You are a fool," he said, hands clenched behind his back. "History will remember you as nothing but a fool, Quorthon. A fool with his little toy gun he created and nothing more. I will move forward without your blessing, then."

"You will do nothing of the sort!" he shouted at Am'ranth, who was already heading toward the door. "You will turn and face me when I'm talking to you!"

"Good day."

"You will face me!"

Am'ranth kept walking, but a tug on his left shoulder stopped him cold in his tracks. He grasped Quorthon's wrist with his right hand, twisting and pushing him back, sending the hulk of a man crashing onto his back, pulseaxe clattering on the ground. The mighty Krigan warrior scrambled to his feet, grasping for the ax, and raced toward Am'ranth, swinging the ax with a wild cut aimed at his skull. Am'ranth's hand sprung up, catching the blow, the ax frozen in place. Quorthon was shouting, turning a deep hue of red and didn't see Am'ranth twist his hips and plant a kick square to his chest with his right leg, sending the Jarl of Krigar crashing back onto the dais, the ax still in Am'ranth's hand.

"History will see you as the fool," he said, tossing the ax aside before turning back toward the door, his cape spinning behind him. There would be no turning back, there would be no peace. Quorthon had made that decision, damning his people to a lifetime of hardship, scorn, war, and unnecessary death.

CYDONIA RISING SAMPLE CHAPTER

00. SPACE GIRL

JACE

Jace leaned back in his chair, carefully resting his bare foot on the console in front of him, doing his best to not trigger anything. The metal chassis felt cold to the touch, but so did just about everything on the ship. It had been seven cycles since Jace had bought the *Pequod* and struck out on his own, yet it still didn't feel like home to him after all of that time. There were a few rooms he had made his own, but they were few and far between. The ship's control deck—a glorified cockpit with room for maybe four people—had always been one of the areas where Jace had gone out of his way to make it feel like it was his.

Those areas that Jace spent time in were always in a constant state of disarray, Jace inhabiting them throughout most of his flight time while ignoring the rest. He knew he didn't always have to be in the control deck while traveling and that autopilot took care of most of the work, but when you flew alone as Jace did, there were fewer and fewer reasons to sprawl out or search for alone time. There was also the neurotic fear of something going horribly wrong and not being close enough to take evasive action thanks to not having a crew to rely on. That being said, most of his voyages were "alone time" by choice.

Jace was selective about what jobs he took, and he stayed away from most of the live cargo or transport jobs. The *Pequod* was up for carrying more people, with plenty of additional quarters and room for at least twelve to live comfortably, but for Jace, his solitary existence was what felt comfortable to him. That meant moving shipments from moon to moon, planet to planet within the Andlios Republic under the rule of Cronus Freeman. Jace snorted to himself at the very thought of Cronus Freeman while he shook his head, picking himself up out of the command chair and stretching his arms out as far as they could go before his hands smacked against a part of the hull. He was hungry anyway and the great expanse that was space whizzing all around him could wait for him to get back. He figured it wasn't going anywhere without him.

Jace plodded down the metal steps into the ship's galley, forced to duck through doorways and sidle through the hallways that were rough on his bulky frame. He was tearing through the compartments looking for something that wouldn't require much of him while sucking on a pack of water. He wore a few days' worth of stubble at most times and his hair was in a constant state of disarray, a light brown mess that he always ran his fingers through. He was hungry and anything would do. Maybe some of that freeze-dried stuff that never quite tasted like what the label said it was, but it didn't require him heating anything up or having to wait for it. That stuff also lasted for years, which was helpful when he was on longer jobs. He'd always pick up fresher foods before he left for a job, but after a few days, it was back to canned food and freeze-dried stuff. At this point, he was just under a week out from Cyngen and he had eaten his last apple two days prior, so freeze-dried was about all that he had left.

He sorted through the packets inside the metal drawer, tossing aside a few before picking out one labeled "Cherry" and slamming the drawer shut with his hip while he held the packet up to his mouth. He gnashed his teeth against the top, trying to tear it open when he heard the alarm from the deck blaring throughout the ship. Great, he thought to himself, he must have miscalculated something or he was on a collision course with an asteroid and certain doom. If Ro were still alive, she'd be lecturing him on being reckless again, and the thought brought an impulsive smile to his face, even with the possibility of certain doom hanging over his head. That was something he wanted to avoid, at least for the time being.

He quickly found himself regretting not wearing shoes while he sprinted down the corridor, up to the metal stairs and into the control deck. Jace slid effortlessly into his chair and slapped a button above the control chair to turn the alarm off, the packet dangling from his mouth. He surveyed the readings only to see that he was rapidly approaching an object in space. It wasn't anything natural, it was man-made and it was definitely too small to be a ship, even a smaller ship. There was also a life sign, which made his heart jump a bit.

Jace quickly entered a few commands and zoomed in on the object, a projection rotating on the left-hand side of the window before him. It was a life pod, a larger one, too. It was large enough to fit multiple people, but his scans were just picking up a lone lifeform in it. They were still deep out in space, about five days away from the Cydonian-inhabited planet of Cyngen near the outskirts of the system. That meant almost two weeks out from Andlios. He was out in no man's land and knew if he didn't stop it, whoever was aboard that life pod was a goner.

With a groan, the ship's HyperMass Drive powered down, Jace watching the space around him turn from streaks to still stars. There was still no visual on the life pod, it being a few klicks out, but his sensors were still reading it. Most life pods didn't have much by the way of comm systems, but he sent through an automated reply just the same, curious as to why the life pod didn't have its distress beacon activated. This was pretty deep in the middle of the frontier, so there was a good chance that whoever was aboard had given up hope and was just waiting for death to come.

The *Pequod* was a smaller class freighter, which gave it higher maneuverability and the ability to be a bit quicker with still enough room in the cargo bay to fit that life pod. With a flick of a switch, the cargo bay door was opening up, a display showing him the door status while he inched closer to the pod. It wouldn't be an easy pickup for most pilots, but for Jace, this was all a part of his job. There were often times where he'd be asked to retrieve lost cargo in remote systems, being hired out by logistics companies who were too embarrassed to admit that they had lost some in a transfer and instead paid him to do the dirty work for them discreetly.

Picking up a life pod from deep space wouldn't be much of a sweat. Jace deployed the cargo arms on each side of the bay doors, controlling them via twin joysticks on the dash. While the *Pequod* inched closer to the pod, he put the arms in motion. The arms reached out, the right grabbing ahold of the pod to stabilize it while the left edged in to get a grip on it. When the pod was firmly locked into place he retracted the arms and waited until his display showed that the pod was secured and then he closed the bay doors.

There hadn't been a visitor aboard with him in at least four standard months, which only made him more self-conscious about the shape of the ship. Jace quickly fumbled for a pair of socks and his boots, slipping the socks on in a hurry and pulling the boots up over his feet, clumsily clomping to his feet and almost tripping over his left boot, which he hadn't fully stepped into yet. He let out a sigh, wondering if he had maybe lost a step when it came to dealing with the human race since Ro passed seven cycles prior.

Jace quickly shook the face of his dead wife out of his head, pulled on his jacket and strapped his pulsepistol's holster around his waist. While it hadn't crossed his mind before, he was now imagining a setup with a life pod floating helplessly waiting for some moron to swoop in to save the day only to find himself in the middle of an ambush. Jace knew how to take care of himself and had a fair amount of practice with a gun, but it was mostly for show just in case someone tried to get the jump on him. The walk down the stairs to the cargo bay was a bit more graceful than his last bout with the stairs, but he had company to worry about.

The meter on the door read that the cargo bay had finished pressurizing and that it was safe to go in, so he took a deep breath and flung the door open, fighting off the chill he felt from the room that just moments before had been exposed to the freezing depths of space. Jace tugged on his jacket, cursing to himself for being a good guy while he stomped over toward the life pod, searching for the door.

"Stay where you are," a voice came from behind him. He

froze in place, his hand moving up toward the pistol holstered by his waist. "Hands up." The voice was confident, unwavering, and very clearly female.

"Okay," Jace raised his hands up slowly. "See, I'm raising my hands. You know, I did rescue you from what seemed like imminent death out there."

"I don't know that yet," she said as Jace felt the barrel of a gun being jabbed into the small of his back.

"I see you aren't one for talking first, just right to the guns and the demands, huh?"

"Look." He felt the tension on his back ease up. "A girl just has to be careful out here in deep space. You aren't a bounty hunter, are you?"

"Bounty hunter?" He laughed. "No, I'd probably make money if I did that. I move cargo." He pointed carefully toward the crates in the cargo hold. "If you'll let me move I'll go and show you the manifest and where I'm heading."

"That could just be a cover."

"Okay," he gulped, trying to find a way to either reach for his gun or somehow talk her down. "You were floating with what my ship read to be about one day's left of life support out here in deep space. I was just trying to be a nice guy."

"I've met my share of nice guys." She grabbed a hold of his arm and pushed him face-first up against the life pod. Her rough gloved hands were patting him down and his pistol slid from the holster. "This the only weapon you had on you?"

"Yeah," he groaned, his face burning up against the cold life pod. "Can you let me go now?"

"Fine." She let go and Jace took a deep breath and turned to face her. She was in her mid-to-late twenties with mid-length blonde hair pulled back into a loose ponytail, which was draped over a leather jacket that hugged her tightly. "But I have some questions."

"You bet that I do as well." Jace rubbed his face, trying to warm it up. "This is the last time I stop for a helpless life pod."

"Yeah, well." She placed her pistol back into a holster on her thigh over her cargo pants, still holding Jace's pointed at him. "I'm not exactly helpless."

"Clearly my mistake," he joked, trying to lighten the mood. "Look, my name is Jace and this ship you are on is the *Pequod*. I'm not sure what you are running from, but you are safe with me for now. I'm heading to Cyngen right now to make a delivery, and you are more than welcome to tag along as long as you stop pointing my own gun at me."

"Why would anyone go to Cyngen?" she asked, looking confused. "Even the Republic barely bothers with them."

"Because I have a delivery to make, that's why." He straightened out his jacket. "Look, it's cold in here, you mind if we head somewhere else where we can warm up? You can point guns at me in any room on this ship, I promise you."

"Fine," she nodded, walking behind him while he headed for the door.

"I didn't catch your name," he said.

"I didn't give it." She jabbed the gun into his back again.

"This isn't a good start to our friendship, is it?" he asked, trying to feel her out.

"Fine," she let out a sigh. "My name is Kat, now can we move?"

"Well, Kat," he said in a sardonic tone while throwing the heavy door open. "It's a pleasure to meet you."

They walked silently through the ship, and any consideration of giving her the full tour was hampered by the gun pointed at him the entire time. They walked through the ship until they came to the galley. Jace pulled up a stool for himself and motioned at the one across the counter from him. She sat down, still clearly on edge. He knew better than to make any sudden movements, but there was another gun hidden in the drawer behind him, he'd just need to distract her to get to it first.

"How about you tell me about yourself, then?" He broke the silence.

"I'd rather not."

"Okay, then, how about how you got here? What's your story?"

"Not much to tell, really." She looked around uneasily, laying his pistol down in front of her, barrel pointed at him. "Things went south and I ended up floating in the middle of space."

"I noticed something on your life pod." He bit his bottom lip, clasping his hands together on the counter. "Other than the fact that it was a pretty big one, I noticed some damage on it. Did you come under fire?"

"You could say that." She stared down at the gun, not making eye contact.

"Not very talkative, I get it, I'm a stranger and all."

"I need to get to Cyngen," she said.

"As I said, that's where I'm heading, you can hitch along if you like, you just can't point a gun at me the whole time."

"I have no reason to trust you."

"No, I guess not," he drummed his fingers on the table absentmindedly, causing her to raise the gun up further. "Oh, sorry, a nervous habit."

She motioned with her head toward his hand. "So where is your wife?"

"My wife?" He looked up at her, puzzled. "Who said anything about my wife?"

"That ring on your finger did." She motioned with her head toward his hand. "Is there anyone else aboard this ship that I need to know about?"

"Oh, right." He found himself absently playing with the ring, twisting it on his finger. "Sometimes I forget that this thing is still there."

"I don't need the whole story, just need to know who else is aboard this ship."

"It's just me," he said. "Just lonely ole' me."

"So she left you, then, huh?" Kat asked.

"No," he hung his head, carefully choosing his words. "She's dead."

"Likely story."

"I'm a lot of things," he said, "but when it comes to my wife I don't joke around."

"Oh. I'm sorry to hear that."

"Oh, you know, it was over seven cycles ago now, I'm used to it. I travel alone now."

"So it's just you aboard this big freighter?"

"Yep."

"Can I have access to your ship's scanner to see for myself?"

"Oh, right. Look, I'm going to reach for my holoscanner right now, but I'm gonna do it slowly so don't think I'm up to anything, alright?"

"Fine," she said. Jace kept his right hand on the table and moved his left to his belt. There was no way he could reach behind him for his hidden gun without her noticing, so he snapped the lock on his holoscanner and placed it down on the table in between them.

"Just..." He began explaining where to find the scanner to her when she snatched it up with her free hand and began tapping away. "So I guess you know where to find the scanner, then."

"I've been around ships my whole life," she said, trying to keep an eye on him while she pulled up the info. "The scan is clean."

"Just like I told you."

"I guess so," she said, slightly lowering the gun.

"See, you don't need that."

"How do I know you don't just make puppy dog eyes at every girl you bring on board with some sob story about your late wife to lower their guard?"

Jace just laughed, letting his guard down.

"Hey, I'm serious here."

"You're a trip," he said. "You've probably seen some shit. My wife is dead, you can trawl through Republic records to confirm it if you want. Because shit, that is something I'd lie about, right? Why not? I'd lie about the only person I ever cared about being dead just to make a pass at some girl I just met."

"Okay, okay, fuck," she said. "I'm so sorry, I didn't mean to..."

"No, no," he said. "It's okay. I understand. I'm just some guy out here, you don't know me from the next goon. I took Ro's death kinda hard and ever since then I've kind of kept to myself out here, making runs on the fringes. I'm not very fond of the Republic either, you know. Nobody making runs on the fringes is getting fat Republic contracts, that's for sure."

"I guess not," she nodded, not making eye contact. "If you don't mind me asking, what happened to her?"

"I do mind," Jace stood up, looking around the galley before finding the packet of cherry protein he had pulled out before, tearing it open and taking a big bite from it. The packet lay right by the drawer where the gun was hidden, but the situation felt like it was diffusing itself, so reaching for it would only make things worse.

"Sorry, I didn't want to pry or anything, was just making conversation is all."

"How about this." He turned to face her, taking another bite of the grainy protein syrup and swallowing hard without really tasting it, not that there was much to taste anyway. "You don't ask about my wife and I don't ask why you are on the run, that sound good?"

"That works for me," she nodded, tapping her fingernails against the cold steel counter.

"Now can I have my damned gun back, already? I promise I won't shoot."

"Erm, well..."

"Look," he said. "There's another gun right here next to me so if I wanted to shoot you I could have already. See?" He slid open the drawer and showed her his spare gun, and she frowned at it and shook her head.

"I guess," she said. "I mean, I still don't know if you'll..."

"If I'll what? This way we'll both have our guns. I promise not to shoot if you don't."

"Alright, alright, fine." She slid it across the counter, and Jace caught it and slipped it back into his holster.

"The charge pack as well," he said as he shot her a mischievous smile.

"You're perceptive, I'll give you that." She reached into her pocket, presenting the small battery pack and sliding it across the counter into his hand. "I'll still be watching you, though."

"I don't know how long you plan on hitching along with me." He slid the battery pack into the handle of his pistol, powering it on and reading the level before placing it back into the holster. "But I've got a few rooms down below, you can pick whichever one you want. I'm sure you are tired after being in a life pod for as long as you were."

"That'd be great, yeah." Kat seemed uneasy still, but at least Jace didn't have to scramble for his hidden gun.

Katrijn

THE QUARTERS aboard the *Pequod* were small but inoffensive. Jace seemed alright enough, but she kept an eye on the door, with her concealed knives and gun in reach just in case. The whole dead wife thing kind of took her for a loop and broke down her ability to keep a gun trained on him, but she didn't exactly trust him just yet. Trust was in short supply for her, especially after what had just happened aboard the *Goliath*. She replayed the last few moments aboard the *Goliath* in her head and shuddered at the thought. She had trusted Rodan and even paid him well enough before a transmission came through from the Andlios Republic. Cronus's power was absolute, after all, and if he wanted her dead that is how she'd end up sooner or later. That journey she had booked to Cyngen had cost her every last credit she had left, but she knew that she couldn't have stayed much longer on Omega Prime after the last sweep from the Republic, considering how close she came to being captured. Rodan had seemed like a good guy until a better offer rolled in.

Life on the run wasn't easy for Katrijn, but it had been all she had known for most of her life. She cursed the name of her brother, Cronus Freeman, night and day for refusing to give up on his relentless search for her. Their father, Jonah Freeman, was the hero of Andlios and had kept the peace for years, but her brother was another story altogether. It was a reign of terror from the beginning, with there even being whispers of Cronus being responsible for their father's death. She knew it in her heart that he had something to do with it, that him accusing her was just an elaborate smokescreen, a way to focus the rage over losing the emperor for the people. The convenient apothecary who claimed she had bought poison from and who Cronus promptly executed was all the convincing she had needed to go into hiding and she was never able to look back.

After a brief nap, she stretched out, checking the charge on her pistol before deciding to do some exploring. Some might call it prying, but she needed to know who she was aboard this ship with. The last time she had trusted someone aboard a ship it turned bloody in a hurry and ended with the ship being blown to bits and her left for dead, floating alone in a luxury life pod. She shuddered. There wouldn't be any luxury life pods aboard this ship, she thought to herself.

She pulled open the heavy door to the quarters, which was mildly obnoxious considering she had come from a ship that was automatic everything, but it was somewhat endearing to be aboard a ship that had some character to it. This ship had nothing but character, although perhaps a bit too much for her liking. Standing on the other side of the door was Jace walking by to his quarters, almost suspiciously.

"Oh, hey," he turned red. "I was just going to read for a bit or something. I had to come up with a new course, but everything is back on track to arrive at Cyngen in about four days."

"Great," she smiled, fixing her hair and straightening out her jacket.

"Hey, since you don't have a gun pointed at me this time, how about I give you a tour? I figure you should be comfortable for the next three days after all, right?"

"That'd be good, yeah." She stretched out. Kat still didn't feel quite comfortable around him just yet, but he was mildly endearing in some puppy dog kind of way. Not endearing enough for her to leave the gun behind, though.

"Well, you already know the quarters down here," he nodded at the door to the room she was staying in. "You've been to the galley and the cargo hold, let me show you to the control deck. Although, fair warning, it is pretty messy."

"That doesn't bother me." She appreciated his honesty, laughing to herself at how he projected the image of a tough loner but that was undoubtedly a front. He did a poor job of hiding how much of a front it was.

"Okay, good." He motioned for her to go in front of him, which gave her pause. She stood frozen, shaking her head, letting him walk in front of her, carefully walking through the narrow hallway to a set of stairs. Most of the ships she had been on that were this size had a lot more of it personalized. You wouldn't find bare metal steps, instead, there would be some level of customization, like even some rough carpeting thrown over it to pad it, but not on this ship.

She stepped up past the last step, walked into what looked like a small lounge only for Jace to come up from behind her. "Yeah, this is kind of a place to hang out or whatever, I'm not sure why it's right by the control deck, but I didn't design this ship."

"It doesn't look like you've done much with this ship at all if I'm honest here," she said. "Looks kind of stock."

"I don't really spend much time in most of it." He scratched the back of his head nervously before running his fingers through his hair. "Pretty much just my quarters and the control deck. The rest of the ship isn't really 'me,' but those two places are. Just look." Jace pulled open the door to the control deck, and Kat had to step back to avoid the door while it moved on its hinges. As the door opened, it unveiled a control deck that was carpeted and littered from top to bottom with books—old, hardbound books—and photos all over the cockpit.

"Wow." She truly felt taken aback at the sight, leaning over and picking a book up off of the ground and thumbing through the pages. "That is a lot of books you have in here."

"I'm shocked you even know what they are." He sat down in the pilot's seat and leaned back. "Most people have only heard of them and have spent most of their lives reading on holoscanners."

"My father was obsessed with books." She found her thoughts drifting, only to shake herself back. Kat looked down at the book, closing it to inspect the cover. "VALIS," she said aloud. "Not sure that I've ever heard of this before."

"It's kind of weird," he said. "It's old, really old. In fact, I'm shocked that it survived this long."

"Especially with it being on the floor in here." Kat looked over at Jace only to find him not laughing. "I mean this is old and valuable and sitting on a pile up here."

"Sure, sure," he threw his hands up. "Rag on the guy for living his life the way he wants to."

"You just said that it was rare." She tossed the book onto the ground back into the pile where she had found it. "Is that how you care for valuables?"

"It's not like it's the last one in existence or anything, or that if the hard copies disappeared it would be wiped from our consciousness. You can find it via holoscanner like everything else in mankind's sordid, confusing history."

"Oh, Freyja. You aren't one of those Mankind Truthers, are you?"

"What?" He looked up at her, puzzled. "No. Look, alright, there are some things that need answers and I'm not sure that—"

"You are, wow."

"Hey, our history is fucked up," Jace said. "I'm not sure where we came from, what came first, you know."

"You mean the chicken or the egg?"

"What?"

"Nevermind." She shook her head. "So is this your play, then? You take a girl into the cockpit of your ship to show her your book collection and your devil may care attitude?"

"My play?" He grimaced.

"You know what I mean." She walked around the cockpit, inspecting the photos along the wall before stopping on one of Jace, looking a bit younger, with a woman. They looked happy together. Katrijn plucked it from the wall, pointing the photo at him. "Is this your wife?"

"Ugh," he groaned, snatching the photo out of her hands and almost bowling her over in the process. He traced his fingers along the hull, finding the exact spot on the wall where the photo was and sticking it back into place, rubbing it a few times with his fingers to ensure that it stayed put. "Do not fuck with those, please."

"I'm sorry," she found herself reaching for her knife at her waist just in case, but holding off. "I didn't mean anything by it, I just…"

"No, it's fine," he took a few deep breaths. "I'm sorry. I just get touchy about Ro's stuff sometimes."

"I understand," she said, thinking back to the spot she found herself in. He seemed harmless enough, but she would feel infinitely more comfortable when she was off his ship and on Cyngen.

"So let's talk about why you are on the run here," Jace stared out the window, fidgeting with a few controls absent-mindedly.

"I thought that was off limits?" She tsked.

"It was," he turned back to her, smirking. "But so was anything about my wife, yet here we are."

She let out a sigh, turning the copilot's seat to face her and sunk down into it. The leather felt cold to the exposed skin of her back while she let the chair envelope her. Katrijn didn't want to give away too much about herself, especially to Jace. He seemed alright and all, but she had learned her lessons the hard way about trusting someone while on the run. The chair turned to face the window, Katrijn gazed out into the abyss, stars streaking past the window like a giant blur of light.

"My father is dead," she started, carefully selecting her

words. "After that happened, everything fell apart. I had a lot of expectations for me, but it was too late for me to fix anything. He was so blind." She had compartmentalized all the trauma from it over the cycles on the run that she was finally able to control her emotions while thinking about it. "He didn't see what was happening. I had to run, I had no other choice but to run. If I stayed, I would have been killed, just like he was. They didn't want me in their way. So I ran."

They both sat in silence, Jace pretending to be engrossed in the readouts in front of him but clearly just trying to avoid saying anything else. She felt bad about making him uncomfortable, but she was so used to being uncomfortable and on edge herself that it came naturally to make any situation she was in a lot worse. If he had known who she was and how much of a bounty was out on her head what would he do? she wondered.

"That's terrible," he finally broke the silence.

"That's life," she tugged her leg up onto the chair, hugging it close to her chest. "What can you do but just deal with the hand you were dealt?"

"Ro was killed by one of Freeman's men," he admitted, the words tumbling out of him clumsily, awkwardly filling up space around them. "She was an activist, rallying against his repealing of the Information Freedom Act that Cronus's daddy dearest had passed before his death. Cronus had them all slaughtered, right there in the street, in front of the whole world to see. We weren't allowed to collect the bodies, they were left to rot out in the streets to leave a message, I guess. I, just..."

He didn't finish his thought, but he didn't need to. Rumors of Cronus's abuses of power had spread throughout the Republic, although many didn't believe them and felt that they were exaggerations. He had many faults and, sadly for Jace, one of those was his affinity for the dramatic. Cronus had a particular disdain for activists and anyone who attempted to undermine him in public. Usually, the families of his victims were given hush money in hopes of them not going to the press. They were forced to sign legally binding agreements that forbade them from speaking publicly about their ordeals, by the punishment of death. She never thought she'd actually meet someone who lived through that, especially not out here.

"So that's how you got the money for this ship." She hugged her leg closer and shivered.

"Yeah," he let out a sigh. "It was her last gift to me. There was a video from one of the reporters that was on the scene..." He paused, looking visibly angry. Jace took a deep breath. "But because I was a coward, because I took the damned money, nothing could come of it. I still have the blasted thing tucked away in my bunk, too."

"I knew it was bad." She rested her chin on her knee. "But not that bad."

"We are all just pawns in Freeman's little game at this point." He stared forward, his eyes fixed on the screens. "That's why I'm out here, that's why I'm away from all of it. I make my living doing odd jobs for people out on the fringes and keep my distance from the heart of the Republic."

"I know what you mean." She bit her bottom lip. "I've been running my whole life. We aren't that much different in that way, I guess. By the way..." She pushed off of the dashboard with her right leg, spinning toward Jace, catching her foot gracefully on the side of his chair to stop her momentum. "What exactly is it that you are delivering anyway?"

"Just supplies, mainly," Jace said. He looked sullen, clearly having some repressed memories stirred up had jarred him.

"Each of the fringe planets are habitable in their own ways, but they all lack a few things that make human life comfortable—or even possible—so what I do is go from planet to planet making deliveries of the stuff they need. So we are headed to Cyngen and while Cyngen has lush forests and wildlife there, for a planet full of Cymages, it lacks any significant source of silicon."

"Really? Silicon?" She said. "So you are transporting a bunch of silicon? I thought that stuff was everywhere and pretty common?"

"It is, but the trace amounts that were on Cyngen have either been used up or it isn't electronic grade. They don't use it for much anymore, and most complex electronics need only small amounts of it, but it's still integral. So I'm coming from Kriyar, which is a desert planet that has an abundance of silicon but doesn't have much fruit. Kriyar and Cyngen have a pretty good system set up where they trade with each other and I'm the middleman. Both sides pay me upon delivery."

"So you just go back and forth between those two planets?"

"Not exactly. I work with about half a dozen planets right now on the fringe that all interact with each other in some way. I'm not the only one who does this, but my reach is probably the widest thanks to the *Pequod* being the ship that she is." Jace reached out and patted the hull of the ship.

"Well, at least you aren't smuggling or anything," she laughed, turning back to the window.

"Who says this is legal?" He shook his head. "It should be, but the Republic tries to have its hand involved in all trade. Thankfully their security out on the fringes is a bit more relaxed than it is in the core."

"That is actually a weight off of me."

"What do you mean?"

"That means that we are both outlaws." She raised an eyebrow at him playfully. "It means that we both have a lot to lose by getting caught. Jace, I think that I might be able to trust you for a while."

"That's good." He scratched his head, looking uneasy. "I guess?"

ABOUT THE AUTHOR

Dave Walsh was once the world's foremost kickboxing journalist, if that makes any sense. He's still trying to figure that one out.

The thing is, he always loved writing and fiction was always his first love. He wrote *Godslayer* in hopes of leaving the world of combat sports behind, which, as you can guess, did not exactly work. That's when a lifelong love of science fiction led him down a different path.

Now he writes science fiction novels about far-off worlds, weird technology and the same damned problems that humanity has always had, just with a different setting.

He does all of this while living in the high desert of Albuquerque and raising twin boys with his wife. He's still not sure which is harder: watching friends get knocked out or raising boys.

facebook.com/dvewalsh

twitter.com/dvewlsh

amazon.com/author/davewalsh

bookbub.com/authors/dave-walsh

goodreads.com/dvewlsh